# Evie the
# Knight

adapted by Maggie Testa

based on the screenplay "Mike the Knight and Evie the Knight"

written by Lisa Akhurst

Simon Spotlight

New York   London   Toronto   Sydney   New Delhi

SIMON SPOTLIGHT

An imprint of Simon & Schuster Children's Publishing Division

1230 Avenue of the Americas, New York, NY 10020

First Simon Spotlight edition March 2015

© 2015 Hit (MTK) Limited. Mike the Knight™ and logo and Be a Knight, Do It Right!™ are trademarks of Hit (MTK) Limited. Nickelodeon and all related titles and logos are trademarks of Viacom International Inc.

All rights reserved, including the right of reproduction in whole or in part in any form.

SIMON SPOTLIGHT and colophon are registered trademarks of Simon & Schuster, Inc.

For information about special discounts for bulk purchases, please contact Simon & Schuster Special Sales at 1-866-506-1949 or business@simonandschuster.com.

Manufactured in the United States of America 0215 LAK

10 9 8 7 6 5 4 3 2 1

ISBN 978-1-4814-2758-6

ISBN 978-1-4814-2759-3 (eBook)

Mike's sister, Evie, was spending the afternoon practicing her magic. "Web of spider, slime of snail, move Mr. Cuddles onto that pail!" she chanted and waved her magic wand.

But Evie's magic didn't go as planned. Instead of moving her frog, Mr. Cuddles, onto the pail, the pail zoomed across the courtyard and almost hit Mike's dragon Squirt!

"Sorry!" cried Evie. "This moving spell is really hard to get right."

"Don't worry, Evie," said Mike. "Magic is hard."

Evie agreed with him. "It is. Not like being a knight where you ride around on a horse all day."

"Being a knight is hard too, Evie," Mike told her. "There's a lot of training to be a knight."

"Well, I think it would be easy," said Evie, and before Mike could stop her, Evie chanted a new spell. "Magic true and magic bright, turn me now into a knight!"

Evie's wizard's hat turned into a knight's helmet. "Look! I'm Evie the Knight!" she said, giggling.

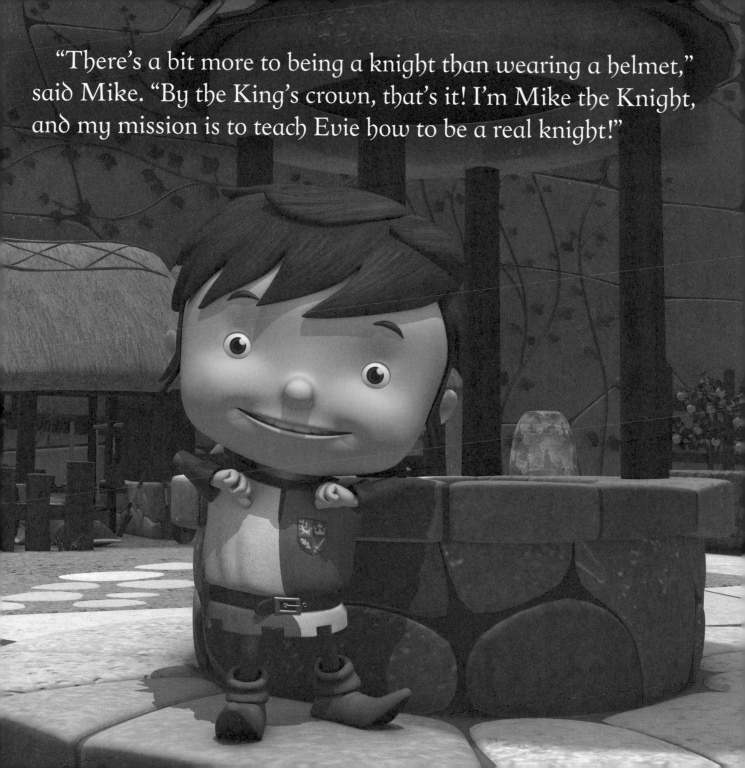

"There's a bit more to being a knight than wearing a helmet," said Mike. "By the King's crown, that's it! I'm Mike the Knight, and my mission is to teach Evie how to be a real knight!"

Mike put on his armor and slid down to the stable to find his horse, Galahad. When he went to pull out his sword, he pulled out a pinwheel instead. But Mike didn't have time to wonder about the pinwheel—it was time to teach Evie how to be a knight!

First, he asked Sparkie and Squirt to be Evie's dragons today.
"Okay, Mike," said Sparkie.

Then Mike began teaching Evie important lessons about being a knight, like protecting the village from Vikings.

"I'll hide and then surprise you like the Vikings would," Mike told Evie.

While Mike found a hiding spot, Evie turned to Sparkie and Squirt. "When I shout 'Vikings,' you do . . . whatever I tell you to do next."

Soon, Mike burst out of his hiding place. "Oog! Aorg! Oog!" he shouted, doing his best Viking impression.

Evie froze for a second, but then she remembered what to
do: She would use the catapult. "Quick, get the sandbags!" she
yelled to Sparkie and Squirt.
"But we don't have any sandbags," replied Squirt.
"Then just grab anything!" instructed Evie.

So Squirt and Sparkie grabbed the nearest things they could find—jam tarts from Mrs. Piecrust's bakery stall.

They loaded them into the catapult, and Evie began launching them at Mike the Viking.
"Evie, what are you doing?" cried Mike.

Soon there were tarts flying all over the village.
Some of the tarts landed near, and some of them landed far . . .

. . . far enough for the *real* Vikings to see them.

The Vikings didn't know where the jam tarts were coming from, but they did know that they wanted more. So they followed the trail.

And the trail led the Vikings straight to the village!
"Quick!" said Evie. "Sparkie, Squirt, scare off the Vikings
with some dragon stuff!"

Sparkie tried to do what Evie asked, but Squirt was too
scared to be scary. All he managed to do was scatter
Mr. Shepherd's sheep. The Vikings weren't going anywhere.

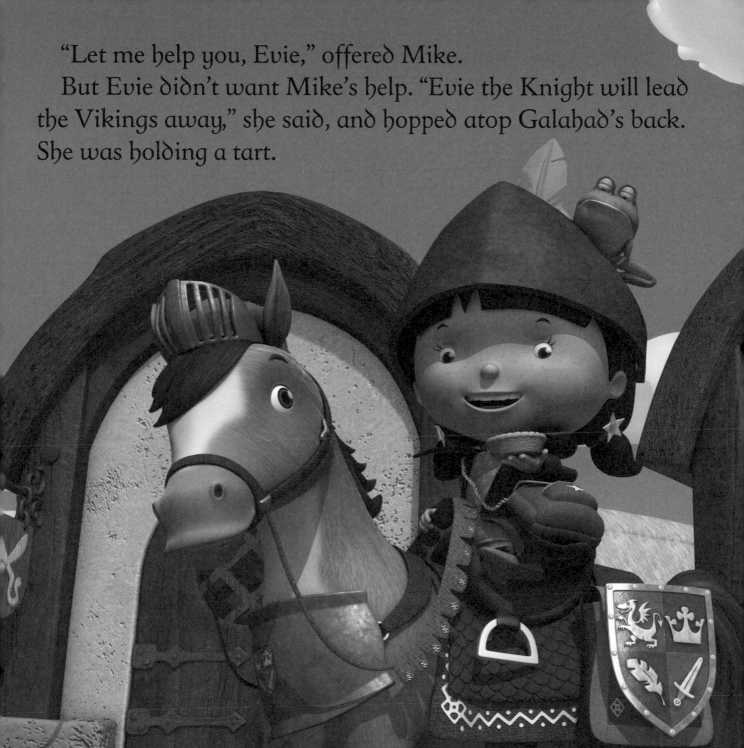

"Let me help you, Evie," offered Mike.

But Evie didn't want Mike's help. "Evie the Knight will lead the Vikings away," she said, and hopped atop Galahad's back. She was holding a tart.

Galahad galloped off. Evie's plan was working—the Vikings left the village and followed her—but she didn't know what to do next.

Luckily, Mike and the dragons had followed Evie as well.
"Throw the tart," Mike told her.

Evie thought that was a good idea. She threw the tart . . .
right to Mike!

Mike caught the tart, but then the Vikings caught Mike.
They carried him back to their longboat!

"I'm sorry, Mike," Evie called after him. "I never should have
said being a knight was easy. It's really hard!"

Evie knew what she had to do. "It's time for me to do it right!" she said. "Let's save Mike."

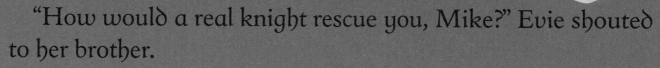

"How would a real knight rescue you, Mike?" Evie shouted to her brother.

Mike took out the pinwheel and tossed it to Evie. "The Vikings love toys. Show them the pinwheel," he instructed.

Evie waved the pinwheel at the Vikings, and it worked! They let Mike go and ran toward the pinwheel. Mike was free. He threw the jam tart toward the Vikings as he got onto Galahad's back.

Evie passed the pinwheel to Grey Beard. While the Vikings njoyed their new toy and delicious jam tart, Mike and Evie made their escape.

Once they had returned to the castle courtyard, Evie gave Mike her knight's helmet. "I'm sorry, Mike," Evie said. "Until you try being a knight, you don't know how hard it is!"

Mike nodded. "We should both stick to what we're best at."

Evie gave Mike a hug. Sparkie piped up. "I'm best at baking tarts!"

Mike laughed. "That's good, because you and Evie have lots of tarts to bake for Mrs. Piecrust!"